# Caillou

# Borrows a Book

Adaptation of the animated series: Anne Paradis
Illustrations: Eric Sévigny, based on the animated series

One morning at day care, Miss Martin read the children a book about animals that live in the ocean. Caillou was very interested because the book showed fish that he had seen at the zoo with Daddy.
"We've finished *Ocean Friends*. Now it's time to play outside," Miss Martin said.

Everyone raced outside, but Caillou stayed behind to ask Miss Martin a question.

"Can I take this book home? I really want to show the fish to my daddy."

"I'm sorry, Caillou. I like to keep our library books here so that we don't lose them," Miss Martin said.

"I'll be really careful with it," Caillou insisted.
"All right, you can borrow it if you promise
to bring it back tomorrow," Miss Martin said.
"I promise!" Caillou exclaimed. "Thank you!"
Caillou knew that he had to take good care
of the book. He went straight to the coat
room to put it in his backpack.

Caillou was just about to put the book in his backpack
when Clementine came into the coat room.
"Come on, Caillou. Let's go play on the swings.
We'll have them all to ourselves," she said.
Caillou followed Clementine outside. He was still holding
the book. Caillou put the book down carefully and
hopped on a swing.

That night at home, Caillou talked about the book
he had borrowed.
"Miss Martin never lends day care books!"
"She must think you're very responsible," Mommy said.
"What does responsible mean?" Caillou asked.
"It means that Miss Martin knows you'll take good care
of the book that belongs to the class library."
Caillou was very proud.
"I can't wait to see those fish," Daddy said.

After dinner, Caillou hurried to find the book.
He searched for it in his backpack. Then he dumped
everything out on the floor. The book wasn't there!
Caillou was in a panic. He ran to Daddy.
"I can't find the book in my backpack!"
"Maybe it fell out," Daddy said. "Let's look for it together."

Daddy and Caillou spent a long time
searching all over the house.
"We've looked everywhere," Caillou said.
"I'm sure the book will show up," Daddy
said calmly.
Caillou sat down on his bed. He felt terrible.
"I'm supposed to take the book back
tomorrow. And I promised Miss Martin
I'd take good care of it."

Caillou felt very sad. He didn't want to disappoint his teacher.

"You know, Caillou," Daddy explained, "being responsible also means fixing your mistakes."

"How can I do that?" Caillou asked.

"Maybe you can think of a way to replace the lost book."

Caillou thought for a minute and then he had an idea.

Next morning at day care, Caillou told
Miss Martin what had happened.
"I'm sorry. I lost the library book,"
Caillou said sadly.
"We looked everywhere, but we couldn't
find it," Daddy added.
Caillou took a handmade book out of
his backpack and gave it to Miss Martin.
"I made this book to make up for the one
I lost."

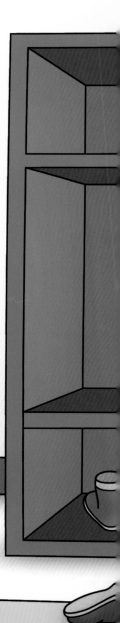

Miss Martin looked through Caillou's book.
"You've done such a good job, Caillou! Thank you.
Come with me, I have something to show you."
Miss Martin took a book from the bookcase.
"*Ocean Friends*! Where was it?" Caillou asked.
"I found it near the swings yesterday."
Suddenly Caillou remembered.
"I'm really sorry. I thought I put it in my backpack."

Caillou hung his head. "I guess I won't be allowed to borrow *Ocean Friends* again."

Miss Martin smiled. "Yes, you will. After this mistake, I'm sure you'll be very careful with the book."

Caillou was so happy that he jumped up and down. "Thank you, thank you! I'll bring it back tomorrow. I promise!"

"And I'll put the new book in our library," said Miss Martin.

Text: adaptation by Anne Paradis of the animated series CAILLOU,
produced by DHX Media Inc.
All rights reserved.
Translation: Joann Egar
Original story written by Karen Moonah
Original Episode #521: Borrowed Book
Illustrations: Eric Sévigny, based on the animated series CAILLOU

The PBS KIDS logo is a registered mark of PBS and is used with permission.

We acknowledge the financial support of the Government of Canada through
the Canada Book Fund for our publishing activities.

Canadian Heritage    Patrimoine canadien

We acknowledge the support of the Ministry of Culture and Communications
of Quebec and SODEC for the publication and promotion of this book.

SODEC
Québec

Bibliothèque et Archives nationales du Québec and Library and Archives
Canada cataloguing in publication

Paradis, Anne, 1972-
[Caillou emprunte un livre.  English]
Caillou borrows a book
(Clubhouse)
Translation of: Caillou emprunte un livre.
For children aged 3 and up.

ISBN 978-2-89718-141-3

1. Responsibility - Juvenile literature.  I. Sévigny, Éric.  II. Title.  III. Title: Caillou
emprunte un livre. English.  IV. Series: Clubhouse.

BJ1452.P3713 2014          j170        C2014-940425-5